KT-362-925

*Thanks to John Cole, who found Sally Brady, who found
Anne Schwartz, who found and loved this book into being.*

To my family of friends in Lelboinet, Kenya
—K. C.

To the African children whose childhoods were stolen
—A. J.

A Note About the Text

For You Are a Kenyan Child is about a day in the life of a Kalenjin boy. Although his first language is Kalenjin, he also speaks Kenya's national language of Kiswahili, also called simply, Swahili. Swahili is commonly heard in villages throughout all of East Africa. Approximately fifty tribes inhabit Kenya, each with their own language and customs. Kenyans speak their own mother tongue, usually another neighbouring tribe's language, *and* Swahili *and* English, both of which they begin studying in Grade 3.

The Swahili used is a casual form of the more correct mother tongue of the Swahili coastal tribe.

In Kenyan villages it is the custom upon entering someone else's compound to call out, "*Hodi?*," the Swahili equivalent of "Anybody home?" Inevitably the answer is the warm reply, "*Karibu!*," which means "Welcome!"

Glossary

Basic Swahili is quite easy to pronounce – people say it is pronounced just the way it looks. *A* is "ahhh," as in "father." *E* is pronounced like a long *a,* as in "play." *I* is pronounced as a long *e,* as in "free." *O* is a long *oh* sound as in "go," and *U* is pronounced like *oo,* as in "boo." The accent is always on the next to last syllable. For example, Swahili is pronounced as Swah-HEE-lee, with the emphasis on "hi" *(hee).*

All words are defined in the story itself, with additional information, when necessary, provided below:

chepati (chay-PAH-tee): common flat pancakes of flour and water cooked in fat on a griddle; often sold in village eating places.

kabisa (kah-BEE-sah): an expression used for emphasis; translates as "exactly."

maziwa lala (mah-ZEE-wah la-la): sleeping milk. Milk is boiled, then left "sleeping" in a gourd hanging on the hut wall until it sours. Then finely crushed charcoal is added to it for sweetening, resulting in a rather lumpy, smoky drink that children like very much.

mzee (mmm-ZAY): term of respect for older people, particularly men.

rungu (RUN-goo): stick used for protection, commonly carried by boys and men; sometimes used as an indicator of importance.

sasa (SAH-sah): now.

For you are a Kenyan Child

Kelly Cunnane
art by Ana Juan

SIMON AND SCHUSTER

Roosters crow,
and you wake one morning
in the green hills of Africa,
sun lemon bright
over eucalyptus trees
full of doves.

For
you
are
a Kenyan
Child

"Hodi?" Anybody home?

"Karibu!" Welcome!

Enter Mama's hut
that smells of earth and smoke.
On a small stool by her fire
sip maize porridge to begin the day,
for you are a Kenyan child.

"Take Grandfather's cows to pasture, my son,"
Mama says. "Watch them carefully."

Into the wild morning wind
you herd the sleepy cows
to the meadow where they graze.

Then – just for a moment – you slip away
to see who else is awake.

"Hodi?"

"Karibu!"

Bashir is opening the tea shop,
red and yellow beanie
on his long loopy hair.
He shakes your hand,
and you shake his,
for this is hello
for a Kenyan child.

He lets you look at him cook.
"*Una taka chepati?*" he asks –
Do you want a pancake? –
and he gives you the first
hot one of the day.

But wait, what's that out the doorway?

A great black monkey hurries by!
Run from the shop to look.
Chase after it!
You want to see!
But the monkey leaps up high
to its home
in the tops of the trees.

You are not watching
Grandfather's cows on the hill,
but you haven't been gone so long . . .
have you?

"Hodi?" "Karibu!"

Inside a little wood shop you peek
and you greet the village chief respectfully.
Jambo, Mzee! Hello, Respected One!

Mzee was once
an African warrior
who hunted lion
and carried
a spear.

He says, "*Una taka shika rungu?*"
Do you want to hold the chief stick?
"*Ndio!*" Yes! you cry, and march proudly
around him, lifting it high.

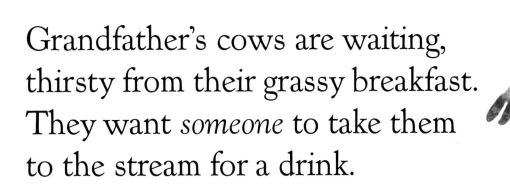

Grandfather's cows are waiting,
thirsty from their grassy breakfast.
They want *someone* to take them
to the stream for a drink.

But look,
who's putting tin dishes
on her hedge to dry?

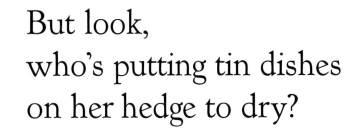

"Hodi?"   "Karibu!"

Grandmother, plump as a hen, smiles and asks,
"Una taka maziwa lala?"
Do you want sleeping milk,
sweetened with crushed charcoal,
fresh from a gourd?

As you drink, Grandmother's knowing eyes
remind you of something
you should do. . .

What could it be?

Oh, no! Grandfather's cows!

Tell Grandmother you are very busy
with your chores,
and hurry away to those cows.

But whose garden of green onions is this,
whose hut under the noonday sun?

"Hodi?"   "Karibu!"

Wini, skinny with soft hair, is laughing,
baby brother tied in a cloth on her back.
Una taka ndudu? Do you want a bug?
And from the sky she offers you one
because they are so sweet.
"Mmmm," you say,
for you are a Kenyan child.

The two of you push gently with your toes
a dung beetle rolling dung
for his home.

"Hodi?" "Karibu!"

Kiptoo, your friend,
the same age as you,
kicks a rag ball by
in the African dust.

"Una taka cheza?"
Do you want to play? he asks.
"Kabisa!" Of course! you shout,
and run without thinking
of anything else
in the world you have to do
but kick the ball
with your friend.

While you catch your breath,
look to the hillside
where Grandfather's cows
always graze –

The cows!
They're gone!

Run to the meadow
you should not have left.
Run as fast as you can,
bare feet over red road,
past women washing clothes,
skinny dogs barking.
Run faster!

The cows must be crashing someone's garden
or standing in the road,
lost at the schoolhouse or gone over a cliff!

Why did you wander?
Why didn't you stay
and do the job Mama
gave you today?

Uh-oh!
There's Grandfather where *you* should be,
on the path with his cows,
going home for evening tea.

Grandfather looks at you,
and you look down.
Then he says, "*Twende nyumbani sasa*" –
Let's go home now –
and he puts your cow switch
back in your hand.

Take the cows home with Grandfather.
Do not stray,
for you are a Kenyan child
and have been everywhere
and seen everything
in this African village today.

Cows sleeping,
rooster quiet,
friends home too.

Curl up in your little hut
near Mama's
and listen closely.
You might hear, among the tall trees,
a great black monkey
telling her child the story
of being chased by a boy,
until they fall asleep . . .

like you,
like us.

SIMON AND SCHUSTER

First published in Great Britain in 2011 by Simon and Schuster UK Ltd.
1st Floor, 222 Gray's Inn Road, London, WC1X 8HB

A CBS Company

Originally published in 2006 by Atheneum Books for Young Readers, an imprint of Simon and Schuster Children's Publishing Division, New York.

Text copyright © 2006 by Kelly Cunnane
Illustrations copyright © 2006 by Ana Juan
All rights reserved
The rights of Kelly Cunnane and Ana Juan to be identified as the author and illustrator of this
work has been asserted by them in accordance with the Copyright, Designs and Patents Act, 1988

All rights reserved, including the right of reproduction in whole or in part in any form

A CIP catalogue record for this book is available from the British Library upon request

ISBN: 978-0-85707-130-9

Printed in China

10 9 8 7 6 5 4 3 2 1